NEVER STOP BELIEVING

25 SHORT INSPIRING STORIES OF AMAZING GIRLS ON GROWTH MINDSET, TEAMWORK, FRIENDSHIP, SELF CONFIDENCE & DETERMINATION

MOTIVATIONAL BOOKS FOR CHILDREN 2

JOHN EBIBI

Love, Mrs. Campbell

EBIBI BOOKS FOR KIDS

CONTENTS

INTRODUCTION

To You, **Amazing Girl**.

What are you aspiring to become in the future? How about your dreams for tomorrow, next week or next month? What is holding you back? Sometimes people think you have to be perfect to achieve your goals. They even believe that if you make a mistake, then you have failed. And for some reason, that mistake signals that you should give up on your dreams.

Instead, mistakes make us better and stronger when we learn from them. The lessons on how to do better next time get us closer to our dream goals. You are a special girl with many talents, so you must remember that. You are going to be faced with lots of challenges. Sometimes you may feel you are not up to the task or things are not going your way and be tempted to give up.

Many people go through the same but what separates the winners is how they manage those challenges. You are part of that winning team. The team of determined, resilient young girls who would not let the world's troubles weigh down their confidence, ambitions or goals.

Why? Because **You Are Amazing,** and you have the power to make a difference for yourself.

This book contains 25 inspirational stories of amazing girls like yourself. It is a powerful and unique storybook covering themes across growth mindset, teamwork, friendship, self-confidence and determination. These are diverse moral lessons and life stories carefully crafted to inspire and positively develop your social skills.

The stories are intended to spark your imagination on approaching similar situations with a positive mindset, enhancing your engagement and learning. We live in an increasingly diverse world, so across these inspirational stories, you would also gain exposure to characters from different geographies and cultures and how they navigated challenging life situations, some of which are fiction scenes.

Inspiration for some of the stories came from my childhood in Africa, so it has a blend of scenes covering Western and African Cultures. So you would get lessons to embrace the diversity of your peer groups and cultures, to motivate you to build your self-confidence, overcome fear and show kindness to others.

You will find an illustration with some of the stories. Feel free to color them to show your creativity and imagination to bring them to life. This way, you would be better immersed in the stories and key learnings, so you never forget them, even during the most challenging childhood moments.

I wish you a pleasant read and hope you are genuinely inspired, and that's because **You Are Amazing**!

John Ebibi

JUST A LITTLE CRAZY IDEA

*E*ver since Remi heard that her great-grandfather and her grandfather were pianists, she also wanted to play the piano. She convinced her dad to sign her up for piano lessons. Remi was excited each time it was piano class. She would pay attention to the musical notes and play as instructed. Remi kept playing and practising and gradually improved, but she wasn't an expert.

One day, she heard that her school was organizing a talent show.

'I am still learning and do not think I will do well,' she said. However, when Remi got home, she thought about it and asked her dad if she could participate. 'If you want to do it, then you should go for it,' her dad said.

But when Remi told her friend about the talent show, her friend did not support her.

'You can't do it; you are not even a perfect pianist; that is a crazy idea,' her friend said. 'Just a little crazy. I think I can do it,' she said.

She practised for the talent show and was confident she could do it. When Remi saw the list of pianists participating in the talent show, she got scared.

'Great grandpa and grandpa were great pianists, I also love the piano, and I can do it,' she encouraged herself.

'Don't be scared, Remi, forget that it is a competition and enjoy the sound you create; play like you are the only one in the room,' her dad encouraged her.

Remi took a deep breath, giving it her best shot when she was called. The judges pointed out where she needed to improve and applauded her performance. Remi was glad when she came in third place in the competition.

'If I keep practising, I will do better,' she told herself as she admired and held on tight to her third-place bronze trophy.

THE END.

AMARI'S BIG THOUGHTS

*I*t's a bright Friday morning in May; Amari looks through the car window as her mom drives her to school. She watches the trees as they drive past the familiar street. Amari had known some of those trees in the previous year, and noticed they had grown bigger.

'What will I contribute to society when I become big?' she asked. The trees provided shade and supplied oxygen. She thought about her preschool teacher's mom, who contributed to society by raising smart kids. Amari also wanted to do something when she was grown up, like her mom, but she did not know what she could do yet.

'What are you thinking of?' her mom asked her, 'day-dreaming again?' her mom flashed her a smile. 'I was thinking about how I can give back to society when I am big like you,' Amari said.

'I am happy you want the society to grow, and you know you have a role to play; that is a good mindset. However, you don't have to wait until you are grown before you can do your part in developing the society; you can start now,' her mom said. 'I am too little to make a change,' Amari said. 'No, Amari, you are not too little. No one is too small or too big to make a change,' her mom told her.

'How can I make a difference?' Amari asked. 'The little things you do matter.' Her mom explained that being kind to people and animals, being polite, and even taking care of the environment is a great way to make the world better.

'What difference will one little Amari make?' Amari asked.'You can't make all the difference, but it is good to start doing something great for your community,' her mom encouraged.

Amari liked the idea of doing something for her community, and from that day, she tried to make the world better in her little way, starting with dancing in her ballet club to raise money for her local children's charity.

THE END.

I CAN'T HEAR YOU

Charlotte was six years old, and it was her first day at her new school, so she was so excited.

'Mom, do you think my classmates will like me?' she asked her mom. 'You are smart and amazing; they will love you,' her mom encouraged her.

Charlotte loved her mom. She was her best friend, who always encouraged and told her she could do anything. She told her never to listen to voices of discouragement. When Charlotte got to school, her new teacher introduced her to the class; Charlotte was glad to be there as she paid attention to her teacher. When the teacher asked questions, Charlotte lifted her hand and answered them correctly. The teacher was impressed. Charlotte was eating her lunch when a girl walked up to her.

'Hi, my name is Pepa,' the girl said. 'My name is Charlotte,' Charlotte responded politely. 'Hi Charlotte, I saw how you kept putting your hand up, answering the teacher's questions; showing off! I just came to let you know that Gill, over there, is the best in this class. Na Na Naa Naaa Naaaa... No one can do better than her, so stop bothering yourself to answer the teacher's questions; Gill will be the best in all the exams,' Pepa said.

'Sorry, I can't hear you,' Charlotte smiled. 'You can't hear me, or you don't believe me?' Pepa asked. 'I can't hear you. I don't hear the voice of discouragement,' Charlotte said and excused herself. Charlotte was not discouraged; she studied hard and always paid attention to the teacher.

When tests and exams came, Charlotte did well and even better than Gill, and Pepa was amazed.

'How were you able to do better than Gill?' Pepa asked. 'It is simple; I refused to pay attention to discouragement. When you shut out discouragement and focus on what you want to do, nothing will be able to stop you.' Charlotte told her.

Pepa took her advice, stopped looking down on herself, and began to see improvements in her performance at school.

THE END.

I CAN'T STOP NOW

Kenita had always loved to play basketball from a very young age. She loved the ball and the court. She would choose basketball over anything else and said it was fun and more enjoyable. When Kenita qualified to play in her first real basketball competition, she was excited and over the moon. She was so anxious and kept practising.

On the day of the competition, she was scared and thought that she would not score many points, but her mom and dad were there to encourage her. Kenita scored six points for her team in the competition, and after that round of play, she practised harder and said she wanted to do even better in the next game.

Kenita wanted to be the best female basketballer in Berkshire County. When another opportunity came for a competition, she participated and scored twelve points, yet she was not satisfied; she kept playing and practising. She kept learning all she needed to learn, and she kept improving herself.

She practised with everything around her, and by the third competition, Kenita scored more points than in the previous games combined. She was happy with her performance. 'Kenita, you are a star; now you must stop practising so much,' her friend told her.

'No, this means I should not stop practising until I get to the point I want to be. I can't stop now,' she told her friend. Kenita kept training, and her dad encouraged her to keep playing, whether winning or losing. The more time she spent making herself better, the closer she got to her dreams.

Kenita took her dad's advice and grew to become the best female basketballer in Berkshire County. She was happy her dream had finally come true. 'Don't stop improving yourself,' Kenita said as she collected her medal as the best female player of the season.

THE END.

YAYA AND THE STREAM

*O*nce upon a time, there lived a girl named Yaya. Yaya was bright and beautiful and had a baby sister called Neh. Yaya was from a low-income family. Her parents were poor, her mom was a tailor, and her dad was a carpenter. Her mom used the pieces of materials left from her customer's clothes to make dresses for Yaya and Neh.

They lived in a poor community suburban area, and their only water source was a stream. The stream was quite distant from Yaya's house. Every other day, her mom would carry Neh on her back and together, they would go to the stream to get water for the family.

One day, Yaya's father was working in his carpentry workshop when he had an accident from a hammer hitting his hand.

Yaya's mom tried to treat his hand from home since they could not go to the hospital. Her father was in pain and could not go to work, so her mom had to work longer hours so they could earn money to buy groceries. Since her dad was ill and her mom was busy caring for him, Yaya had to go to the stream alone to get water. Yaya was at the stream filling her water pot, when it began to rain heavily. She gently lifted her water pot to her head and was walking home when she slipped and fell.

The water pot broke, and Yaya sustained a minor injury to her leg. She cried under the rain as she went home wet with a broken water pot. As Yaya walked home, she recognized how hard her mom was working to support her family, and she promised herself that she would work hard to help her family and community given their hardship.

Yaya worked hard at school, and she was successful in getting a scholarship to go to college. She was determined to succeed, and a few years later, Yaya became a senior officer at the Mayor's office. She lobbied for her community to ensure they had a good water supply and an accessible hospital.

She also became a role model and represented many low-income families in her community on many fronts. Yaya was happy that her community was now in a much better condition and that she had played a role in making a difference for many.

THE END.

TWO VILLAGES, ONE REWARD

*O*nce upon a time, a great chief, Chief Acham, ruled over two villages called Baba and Bafor. The two villages were poorly developed, with no water supplies, bad roads and poor school infrastructure. Chief Acham had a dilemma as he had received some community development funding but was unsure about how to prioritize the funding between the villages.

He was torn between which village deserved the project, so he asked one of his Queen Mothers, Mafor, for help. 'Mafor, we have just received some money from the community fundraising; I am undecided about which of the villages is the most deserving of the new water development project. Which one do you advise me to develop?' the Chief asked.

'I advise you to develop the cleanest village. That way, we will be sure that the new water system will be maintained and properly managed, so we have constant clean drinking water,' Mafor said. Chief Acham agreed it was a good idea, so he called all the quarter heads from the two villages and told them his plan.

'I intend to develop only one village in this first phase, so I have thought of a way to choose the village that deserves it.

The cleanest village will be developed, but I will not tell you the day I will come for the inspection,' the Chief said.

The two villages decided to do all they could to get the Chief's award. Village Bafor all went home and cleaned their homes. As for Village Baba, they called a meeting where they agreed to come out every morning and clean the streets and their homes.

In Village Bafor, they cleaned their homes, but no one came out to clean the streets; everyone assumed the other person would clean the street. On the inspection day, the Chief came very early, unannounced. When he went to Village Bafor, every home was clean, but the streets were not clean, the fields were overgrown, and the trash bins overflowed. The Chief was not impressed.

*W*hen he got to Village Baba, the streets were not completely clean, but he saw everyone working. The men were trimming the lawn and sweeping the streets. The children were singing and keeping them entertained with their drums and local bottle music. The women served their latest harvest of grilled corn.

'We have lost the award, as we were not done cleaning when the Chief came,' some women in Village Baba said. Village Bafor thought they would win the award because their homes were clean during the inspection. On the day of the announcement, the Chief called the two villages and made his pronouncement of the winner.

'Although the homes of Village Bafor were clean, Village Baba was not complete during the assessment. However, the project goes to the Village Baba, as when I did my inspection, I saw teamwork in action and a true community spirit for a common purpose. If they can come together to clean their environment without assuming other people would do it, then I am sure that when the village is developed, they will work together to take care of it,' the Chief said.

Village Baba was super excited that their collective effort had paid off. In true community spirit, they offered help to Village Bafor. The Chief promised Village Bafor they were next in line for other development projects and encouraged them to learn the community and team-building approach from Village Baba.

THE END.

JULIA AND THE COAT

*O*nce upon a time, there lived a girl named Julia. Julia was bright and pretty. Her family could not afford to buy a new coat for her and her sister each winter. During winter, Julia and her sister would be cold and have to manage their old, outgrown coats.

One day, Julia decided to go into the woods and get some wood for the fire so her family would be warm at night. As she gathered wood, she saw an older woman gathering wood for herself. The woman could not lift her wood and asked Julia to help her raise it to her head. Instead of Julia lifting the wood to the older woman's head, Julia lifted it to her own.

She offered to take it to the woman's house before returning to get her wood. The woman was happy and kept thanking

Julia for her help. When Julia got to the woman's house, she saw that the older woman had knitted some coats. Julia admired the coats in different sizes, colors and designs.

'Take as many as you want,' the old woman said. Julia could not believe it. 'Are you sure? I would love one for my dad, mom and sister,' Julia said. She did not want to add one for herself because she felt asking for four coats would be too much. The woman smiled and asked her to make her choice. Julia showed her what she wanted, and the lady packed them.

Julia was excited and did not return for her wood; instead, she ran home to tell her family about what had just happened. When she opened the bag to give them their coats, she found an extra one, she picked it up and saw her name written on it, it was the most beautiful coat she had ever had.

Julia was happy that she and her family had new coats and would be warm for the rest of the winter. She shared her story with her family, and her parents were very proud of her willingness to help the old lady.

THE END.

THE BROKEN BRIDGE

*B*arbs lived in a small village and passed through a narrow bridge to go to school. Everyone in the village had to go through that bridge. The men and women passed through the bridge to work, and the children used the bridge to get to school. Underneath the bridge was a small river. One night, there was a heavy storm where the river overflowed its banks. The rise in the water made the bridge weak, and it collapsed.

The following day, everyone saw that the bridge was broken. 'What are we going to do?' the people worriedly asked. 'We can rebuild the bridge,' Barbs said. 'No, we can't. We need to wait for the Mayor to come,' some people said. 'If we work together and contribute whatever we can, we will rebuild the bridge in a few days if the Mayor or his contractors haven't shown up. We can all return to our businesses, and the other kids and I can return to school,' Barbs said.

Everyone agreed that it was a good idea. Barbs got a jar and went around to collect money for the bridge repair. The contractors showed up and got to work, and the other villagers assisted in any way they could. Everyone got involved in rebuilding the bridge, given how much it impacted them.

Some carried supplies, some water, and some women cooked food and shared snacks with everyone. Everyone was happy as they worked. The children also danced and sang to entertain the people as they worked. After a full day of work, the bridge was reconstructed. Everyone was happy.

The villagers learned that teamwork could make a challenging task much easy. That night, they made a big fire to celebrate their achievement. The bridge was completed, and now they could return to their businesses, and the kids could return to school.

THE END.

FRI'S SACRIFICE

Fri was nine years old, and she was the eldest of her siblings. Fri had two brothers and two sisters. Her father was a fisherman, while her mother was a trader. Fri went to a local school in her community, and her parents could only pay her fees but could not afford to buy her books, and this made Fri sad.

Some days, they would go to bed hungry; other times, she and her parents would not eat, so her younger ones would eat. Fri was unhappy about the condition of things at home, so each time she returned from school, she looked for ways to raise money to support her parents.

Fri would take out the trash for people, water their plants, walk their dogs, wash her neighbor's cars and run errands. In exchange, they would give her some money. Fri kept doing these for some weeks. And any money she got, she would give to her parents to pay her siblings' fees or buy food for the household.

One day, Fri was cleaning the house of a wealthy man. On cleaning the chairs and tables, she found money under one of the couches. She took the money and returned it to the man. 'Thank you, you are an honest girl,' the man said.

Fri continued cleaning the house, and when she finished and was about to leave, the man paid her twice what she was owed. She thanked him and went home happily. But unknown to her, the man was following her. He found out where she was living and saw the poor state of their livelihood.

He later turned up at their doorstep and offered her father employment as his driver and her mother a role as his kitchen staff. He gave them a better house and sent her siblings to a better school. The family was grateful.

Fri took a life lesson that the simple action of honesty had changed their lives forever. She was happy that she and her siblings could now live better lives.

THE END.

CHRISTMAS UNDER THE COLA NUT TREE

It was a dusty Friday morning; Lum was excited because she would go to Baba, where her father had a ranch house for Christmas. Her uncles and aunts, as well as her cousins, would also be at the ranch house. Her father had told her fantastic stories about the ranch and how special it was to spend Christmas under their local 'cola nut' tree.

Cola nut trees were a particular type of tree with a history in the village. So they were precious. Lum looked forward to seeing them. They arrived at the house two days before Christmas. Lum was excited to see her grandparents and other relatives. Lum did not find something appealing. 'Why are there no Christmas decorations?' she asked.

Her grandparents did not see the need for it. Her uncles decided they could have Christmas without decorations. They preferred their traditional rituals of drinking white wine in cow horn cups, sitting around the fire, eating grilled corn and dancing to the local bottle music. Lum was not convinced and was adamant about making it extra special.

'If we work together, I am sure we can have some decorations in time,' Lum said. So she got into the old storage cabinet and brought down the Christmas tree, lighting, and accessories. She assigned roles, and they worked together in decorating the tree and the house, and by Christmas Eve, the tree and house felt like Christmas.

'Something is still missing,' Lum said. 'The gifts and prezzies!' her little cousin, Fru, shouted happily. 'That's for Father Christmas to bring gifts, only if you've been a good girl throughout the year', her Uncle Cho responded. Lum wasn't too happy and reluctantly went to bed, worrying about whether she would have any gifts.

'Wake up, wake up, it's Christmas.' Lum knocked on each door on Christmas morning. Everyone came out in their pyjamas and ran to sit by the Christmas tree, and ho ho ho were there lots of gifts. Lum was super excited and couldn't stop smiling. They exchanged gifts and unwrapped them, smiling as they saw what was behind the wrap. Lum was elated to see happy faces, and she was grateful as they were

able to work as a team to make Christmas special.

THE END.

CORA SAVES THE DAY

Cora was nine years old; she was smart and hardworking. Cora liked to help people and put smiles on their faces. She also loved singing, dancing, and trying new styles on her hair. She would watch videos on hair styling and practise them on herself and her dolls.

Cora had a friend called Elodie. Cora and Elodie loved to do things together; sing duets, dance, go swimming and ballet lessons together. Elodie had long hair, but she never liked her hair because it was thick and gave her trouble maintaining. A few days before Elodie's birthday, Elodie's parents and brother were setting up for the event.

Her mom got ingredients for food and cake, while her dad got drinks and items to decorate. The food and the decorations were set for Elodie's birthday; however, there was one problem. The professional hairstylist who was booked to style Elodie's hair didn't show up, and there was no one to make Elodie's hair look beautiful. She stayed in her room and began to cry.

Soon, there was a knock on the door, and it was Cora. 'Hi everyone, where is the birthday girl?' Cora asked. 'She is in her room crying, and her hair is a mess,' Elodie's brother said. Cora ran home and got all her hair products and accessories. She ran back to Elodie's house and went up to her room. 'Hello, Miss Elodie, I am your professional hairstylist for today, and I am here to make you look like a pretty princess,' Cora said, and Elodie laughed.

Cora dried Elodie's tears and worked on her hair. 'Look at the mirror,' Cora said when she was done. 'Oh wow, Cora, thank you, I love it, babe,' Elodie said and hugged her friend.

She happily went downstairs, and the house was full of guests. Everyone gave compliments about her hair, and Elodie could not stop smiling.

After her birthday, Cora taught Elodie how to take care of her hair, and since then, Elodie never had hair trouble again.

THE END.

THE INVISIBLE FRIEND

*O*nce upon a time, there was a girl named Eva. Eva liked to be alone. She would not talk to anyone at school, and at home, she would lock herself in her room. 'Eva, you need to have friends. You can speak to the neighbor's children or your classmates at school,' her mom would often say.

'I am not alone, I have a friend, and I don't need more friends,' Eva would say. 'What is her name?' her mom would ask. 'Joyce, her name is Joyce,' Eva would say. 'So where is Joyce, you call your friend?' her mom would ask her. 'She is with me, but you can't see her,' Eva would respond.

'I am talking of a real friend, not an invisible make-believe friend,' her mom would always say. But Eva would not listen. Whenever Eva played alone, she pretended to be talking and responding to Joyce, her make-believe friend. 'Joyce, please pass me the comb,' she would say and pick it up herself.

'Thank you, Joyce,' she would say again. One day, Eva was walking home from the grocery store when her paper bag broke, and the groceries fell off. No one was there to help her. She had to manage on her own. As she tried to gather her fruits and manage the torn bag, she wished she had a real friend because Joyce could not help her.

Friends make the world a better place to live in. Eva saw the relevance of having real friends. She started talking to her classmates and neighbors and discovered they were friendly. They were always ready to help her when she needed their help. Eva learned that she needed people; everyone needed someone they could count on.

THE END.

WHERE IS KENA?

*K*ena and Kemi were best friends and liked to do activities together. One day, they decided to go to the park for a picnic. They wore the same yellow dress with a blue flowery pattern. The park was full of families and kids when they got there. The girls held each other's hands and began to have fun.

They stopped at the playground to play games but got carried away and let go of each other's hands. 'Kena, let's go and get ice cream,' Kemi said, but Kena did not respond to her. She looked left and right, but Kena was not beside her. She got worried and wondered where Kena had gone to.

'Where is Kena? How do I find her in this busy park filled with people?' Kemi asked herself. She went around in search of her friend. 'Excuse me, please, have you seen a girl about my height wearing a similar dress as mine?' Kemi asked around. She kept searching and looking for her friend, but she could not find her.

'Where is Kena?' she asked. She was scared and worried. After a long time of searching, Kemi got tired and sat on a bench. She covered her face in her palm and cried. Someone touched her shoulder, and she looked up. 'Kena,' she screamed and jumped up to hug her.

'Where were you? I was worried?' Kemi asked Kena. 'While you were busy playing the ring game, I decided to go and get us drinks so that we could have it when you were done playing, and I didn't want to distract you. I got drinks for us; I'm sorry,' Kena said.

'I don't care about the drinks; I am just glad I have found my friend,' Kemi said happily and wiped her tears.

THE END.

A FRIEND IN NEED

Telma lived in a small village, called Bali and attended the local primary school. She loved her teachers, paid attention in class, and always did well in all subjects except Maths. This bothered Telma, as she would put a lot of effort into studying, but she never seemed to get good results.

One day, Telma sat by the lawn and looked sad. Her friend, Afa, who lived next door, walked up to her. 'What is wrong, Telma? You look sad,' Afa said. 'I am having a problem with Maths; I try hard, but I never seem to get it right.' Afa felt pity for her.

'I could teach you, as I do well in Maths,' Afa offered. Telma was so happy about the offer of help. Each time she returned from school, she spent time studying with Afa. Afa helped with whatever Telma could not understand. This went on for a while, and after some time, Telma began to get better results in Maths.

She learned more about her challenging areas, and she continued to improve. She no longer performed poorly in Maths. One day, Telma went to Afa's house to thank her for helping her get better at Maths. When she got there, she saw Afa looking sad.

'What is wrong?' Telma asked her. 'I need to go to a birthday party today, but my shoe doesn't fit anymore,' Afa said sadly. Without saying a word, Telma ran home; she asked her mom if she could give one of her shoes to Afa, and her mom accepted.

This was possible because the friends were willing to help each other. Telma picked up her favorite shoe and went to give it to Afa. 'This is for you,' Telma said. 'Thank you very much; it is beautiful,' Afa said.

Afa was happy that she had a beautiful shoe at the birthday party, and Telma was delighted that she was better at Maths.

THE END.

FRIENDS FOREVER?

Mona and Aria were best friends, and they did a lot of activities together. They loved the same food, snacks, drink, color, songs and TV shows. They attended the same school and sat together in class. They told themselves that they would be best friends forever.

One day, Aria fell ill and could not go to school. Mona promised to pay attention in class, and when she returned from school, she would teach Aria all she had learned. Mona was bored at school because she missed Aria. When she got home, she told Aria all she had learned from what she could remember.

The next day, Mona was alone again. However, a new girl came to the class, and the teacher asked her to sit with Mona. Her name was Janet.

Mona and Janet spoke to each other, and they got along well. When Aria got better and returned to school, she was unhappy that Mona had a new friend. She felt betrayed. Aria stopped talking to Mona and was angry that Mona had replaced her with Janet.

One day, Aria was walking home from school, and Mona ran after her. 'Aria, I want to talk to you,' Mona said. 'Don't talk to me. Go and talk to your new friend,' Aria said.

'You are also my friend,' Mona said. 'Janet is your new friend; you replaced me with her, even after you promised me we would be friends forever,' Aria said sadly.

'Aria, you are my friend forever. I did not replace you with Janet,' Mona explained. 'But she is your friend,' Aria argued. 'Yes, she is my friend, and you are also my friend. It's okay to have more than one friend,' Mona said.

We should not push others away but embrace them and be friends. Aria realized she was jealous because she thought Janet would take Mona away. She learned that she could be friends with others even if she had a best friend. The bigger the circle of friends, the happier they were. She also became friends with Janet, and they all walked home daily.

THE END.

ASIA, THE STAR BAKER

*A*sia liked to bake, and as her grandma Tish was a baker, she always wanted to assist her in baking. She dreamt of becoming a five-star baker when she was older. One day, Asia decided to prepare the mixture for the apple pie the family would have for dessert.

She did this to surprise her grandma, Tish. When her grandma returned, she helped Asia put it in the oven and decided to give Asia's self-made apple pie a chance. When it was time for dessert, Asia cut out slices for her parents, grandma, and older sister.

'I hope you all enjoy it; I made it myself,' Asia smiled as she served them. Her parents took a bite and commended her; however, her sister was not impressed.

'This is not quite great Asia, and it tastes like paper; next time, you should leave baking for people who know how to bake; you can never be a baker,' her sister said.

Asia was sad; she cried and said she would never bake again. When Asia slept at night, she dreamt she had a big bakery and made the best cakes in the local town of Maidenhead. When she woke up, she decided that her sister's words would not stop her from achieving her dream.

Asia did not give up on her dream of becoming a five-star baker. She looked at the apple pie recipe and saw where she had made mistakes; she kept practising until she got it right and had better feedback from her sister.

Whenever she baked something unpleasant and felt discouraged, she would remember her dream and keep learning. She kept learning to bake new desserts and started writing her recipes as she grew up. Soon, Asia became an excellent baker, recognized by her friends, school and family. She was yet to attain being a five-star baker, but she knew she would get there one day.

Asia built her profile as a baker by baking for charity events for her school and community. She was confident that owning her local bakery one day was achievable, given the relationships and credibility she had built.

THE END.

NOT GOOD ENOUGH

I am not good enough, Georgie said to her teacher. Georgie was an intelligent girl; she was excellent at spelling words, she liked to spell, and she also loved learning new words. Her favorite way to learn faster was to skip a rope while spelling. Her school had qualified for the local spelling bee competition, and Georgie was selected to represent the school and win the award.

However, Georgie doubted she could do it; she told the teacher she could not do it, and when the teacher asked her why she felt she could not do it, Georgie said she was just not good enough. 'Don't say that, don't ever look down on yourself. The world believes what you believe about yourself. Believe in the best of yourself always,' her teacher encouraged her.

Georgie was scared that if she went to the competition, she would not know how to spell what she was asked. She was worried she would not do well, and the school would lose the reward; she didn't want to be the one to make her school fail. Her parents, teachers, and the principal tried to convince her to go for it. They told her she could do it; she needed to believe in herself, but Georgie refused.

Someone else was then chosen to represent the school. On the day of the competition, Georgie was there to watch. For every word that was asked to be spelled, Georgie knew them. However, her school's representative didn't know most of them, and she gave the wrong spellings to the words pronounced, which made her school miss out on the top award.

This pained Georgie, 'if only I had been confident enough to do it,' she said. From that day on, Georgie decided never to allow doubt to limit her from doing what she loved, even if she was scared.

THE END.

I DON'T WANT TO FALL

Kyra had always loved riding a bike, and she would stand and watch in amazement as kids her age rode their bikes around the block. She even had a favorite bike model, but Kyra got scared when her dad got her favorite bike for her birthday.

'Why are you scared? I thought you would be happy to have a bike,' her dad said. 'I am happy to have a bike, dad, but I am scared,' she told him. 'Scared of what?' he asked her. 'I am scared of falling,' she said. Her dad told her he would hold her and not let her fall.

On the first day of her bike lesson with her dad, Kyra wore her safety helmet and climbed on the bike, but she refused to take her legs off the ground. 'Lift your legs, Kyra, and place them over here,' her dad said. 'No, I don't want to fall,' Kyra cried. Kyra was too scared to try, so she could not learn anything. 'Kyra dear, I know you are scared of falling, but you need to speak to yourself, tell yourself that even if you fall, it is part of the process. I will be with you until you can go on your own, but you need to make up your mind first,' her dad assured her.

Kyra made up her mind to face her fears and learn to ride her bike, 'I am ready,' she told her dad. He made her understand that she needed to build confidence to face her fears; if not, she would not be able to learn to ride her bike.

As her dad taught her, she was scared, but she did not let fear get in the way of what she wanted, she kept learning, and even when she fell, she got up and continued riding her bike until she got better.

THE END.

THE MAGIC MICROPHONE

*O*nce upon a time, there lived a little girl named Kelsie. She was beautiful and had a fantastic voice; however, she was shy; she never liked to sing in front of people or on a stage, and she was scared of the microphone. Kelsie loved to sing, she dreamed of singing in front of people, but she did not dare to face the crowd.

One day, the school she attended had a big event, and they asked Kelsie to sing at the event. 'Kelsie, your teacher said you refused to sing at the big event; why did you?' her mom asked. 'I am scared, mom; what if they laugh at me? What if my voice is horrible?' she asked. 'Kelsie, you have a wonderful voice, and no one will laugh at you,' her mom encouraged her. 'You are saying that because you are my mom, others will make fun of me,' Kelsie was worried. 'No, Kelsie, everyone thinks you are amazing,' her mom said.

'What if my voice sounds awful on the microphone?' Kelsie was not brave enough, so she made up various excuses.

'I have a magic microphone, it looks like an ordinary microphone, but it has magic in it; no matter how your voice sounds, when you use this microphone, your voice will be amazing,' her mom said and gave her the magic microphone.

Kelsie was not scared on the day of the big event; she faced the crowd and sang beautifully. Everyone cheered for her. Kelsie was happy, 'mom, the microphone is magical; everyone loved the singing.' Kelsie said to her mom after the event.

'Can I tell you a secret?' asked her mom. 'Yes, mom,' she said. 'It was not the microphone that made people cheer; it was you. The microphone was not magical; it was just an ordinary microphone,' her mom revealed.

Kelsie opened her mouth wide, and she was shocked. She didn't need a magic microphone to give her the courage to face the crowd, and she could do it; all she had to do was believe in herself the way she had thought in the microphone. Kelsie hugged her mom.

From that day, she was unafraid to face the crowd and sing.

THE END.

HEAD: GOOD IDEA: TAIL: BAD IDEA

Sofia was lying in bed one day when she got an exciting idea. Her school was preparing for a graduation party, and they were not sure of the theme for the graduation. She got a vision for the theme but was unsure if it was good.

'I don't think it is a good idea; they would not like it,' she said and pushed the idea aside, but it kept popping into her head. 'Fine, I will throw a coin; if it is head, then it is a good idea, and I will share it, but if it is tail, then it is a bad idea, and I will not share it.'

Sofia got up from the bed and picked a coin from her cabinet. She tossed the coin, and it showed tail. 'I said it; it is a bad idea,' she threw it again, and it showed tail, so she decided not to share the idea.

The next day at school, everyone sat to think about the theme for the graduation, everyone made suggestions, but they were not good enough.

The idea from the previous day kept popping up in Sofia's head. She got tired of pushing it away and decided to share it; after all, there was no harm in communicating an idea.

She shared the idea of getting parents to join in the children's end-of-year performances on stage; everyone was quiet when she was done talking. 'I shouldn't have said anything; now they are all going to laugh at me,' she said.

All of a sudden, everyone began to clap for her. 'Beautiful,' 'I love it,' 'why didn't you share it earlier as it would be fun to see my mom and paps on stage, ha ha ha?' They said you would have saved us the stress of thinking hard. They loved the idea and went with it.

On graduation day, the kids had memorable and priceless moments with embarrassed parents performing musicals with their children. Sofia was glad she spoke up.

From that day, she always decided to share her ideas even if she was unsure how good enough or crazy they were.

THE END.

LEFT AND SPECIAL

*O*nce upon a time, there lived a girl named Karis. Karis was left-handed. She wrote with her left hand and did most things with her left. Karis liked to play basketball. However, she would always miss the net and hardly scored points. This made her sad, 'if only I were right-handed,' she would murmur.

One day, Karis was walking past a basketball court when she saw some players, she stood to watch them, and as she watched them, she wished she was right-handed. She tried to play with her right hand, but she still missed. This made her stop playing basketball. Whenever she came across people playing basketball, she would be sad and murmur, 'if only I were right-handed.'

She kept watching the game and noticed that one player scored over fifteen points. Karis was thrilled, and this player was good at the game. She looked closely and saw that the player was left-handed. Karis could not believe what she was seeing. She decided to wait until the game was over.

After the game, she asked the player, 'please excuse me, are you left-handed?' she asked. 'Yes,' the player answered. 'How is it possible that you are good at the game? I thought it was only right-handed people that play basketball so well?' Karis asked.

'The hand you use does not determine if you are a good player; you need to put in more practice, and with consistency and effort, you will get better,' he said.

Karis took the advice and resumed playing basketball; she kept missing points but didn't give up. With time, she got better and began to score points. Karis was happy as she realized that she could do anything if she put her mind and effort into doing it.

THE END.

I HATE MATHS

*M*aggie was a beautiful girl; she liked to read, dance, and have fun. She also liked to go to school, but she hated Maths. Maggie often had low grades whenever she had a Maths quiz or exam. This made her teacher and parents show concern.

'Maggie, what seems to be the problem?' Her mom showed concern that you do well in other subjects, except Maths. 'Nothing, mom, I just find it difficult to understand Maths; it is hard.' Maggie said. 'No, Maggie, Maths is not hard; you can do it, you can get an A in it,' her mom encouraged her.

Maggie tried to pay attention when her teacher taught, and she tried to practise independently. However, she was still having difficulty with it. One day her teacher called her,

'Maggie, what do you like?' her teacher asked her. 'I like chocolate, dancing, and reading,' she said.

'What about Maths? Do you like Maths?' her teacher asked. 'No way, I hate Maths!' Maggie said firmly. 'Why do you hate Maths?' her teacher asked. 'It is difficult, and no matter how hard I try, I still fail,' Maggie said. 'That is the problem, and if you hate a thing, you will find it difficult to see its beauty. And the more you say something is hard and you can't do it; you will not be able to do it,' her teacher explained.

She encouraged Maggie to stop thinking Maths was hard. 'Imagine that Maths is like a dance; you learn the steps, listen to the music, and you will find yourself dancing easily,' her teacher said. Maggie took to her teacher's advice, stopped hating maths, and stopped telling herself it was difficult.

With time her parents and teachers helped her see some fun ways to learn Maths, and Maggie was determined to be better in Maths, and she became better. In the following Maths quiz, Maggie had a B grade. She never hated Maths again, believing she could be better at it.

THE END.

EXCUSES AGAIN?

*Z*ina liked watching people swim, their body movements, the swimsuits, the goggles, and just the whole setting. 'Mom, please, could you enrol me in a swimming lesson?' she asked her mom. 'Are you sure you want to learn how to swim?' her mom asked.

'Yes, mom,' Zina said. Zina was excited when her mom registered her for swimming lessons the following day. When it was time to go into the water, Zina wore her swimming suit and goggles. She paid attention as the coach provided instructions and the safety procedures.

The coach asked all the learners to line up, and she guided them into the water one after another. Zina got scared when it was her turn. 'Hold on; I want to pee,' she said and excused herself. When she got back, she stood at the rear of the line.

'Come on, Zina,' the coach urged her, but she stayed back. 'I want to watch others today, and I will swim tomorrow,' she said. The following day when it was time for Zina to go into the pool, she made up another excuse, 'My stomach hurts; as soon as I feel better, I will join,' she said.

'Excuses again,' the coach said. 'No, I am not making excuses, I want to learn how to swim, but I am not ready,' she said. 'What are you scared of?' her coach asked her. 'The water,' she said. Zina was willing to try.

Her coach held her hand and helped her into the water, guided her, and started learning how to swim; soon, she forgot about her fears and began to enjoy the water.

The coach told her she would be beside her throughout the learning process until she could do it independently. She encouraged her, and it built her confidence. In a few weeks, Zina became an excellent swimmer and was no longer scared to get into the water.

THE END.

DANCE OR GO HOME

*R*osie, sit still,' her teacher said for the fifth time that morning. Rosie was always moving. She would move her body around if she were standing, and when she sat, her legs would be all over the place; sometimes, her legs made noise on the floor, distracting others. Rosie did not know why she had moved so much. 'Maybe she is just being overly active,' her mom said.

'Rosie, could you stay still for a while?' her mom would ask when she wanted her to hold something or when she was dressing her hair. Rosie would try to keep still, but in a few seconds, she would move again. Her mom got tired and took her to a therapist to find out what was wrong with her.

'There is nothing wrong with her. All I see is a great dancer,' the therapist said. Rosie's mom decided to register her in a dance academy. When Rosie started attending the academy, she struggled to learn the dance steps. 'You don't belong here. Go home,' one of the girls told her. Rosie felt sad and did not want to go to the dance academy again.

Still, when she recalled that the therapist said she was a great dancer, she returned to the academy. Each time she was finding it hard to learn a dance step, she would say to herself, 'dance, Rosie, or go home,' she kept pushing hard and began to learn the dance steps.

Soon Rosie started dancing well and in rhythm; she was determined to be a great dancer and kept practising until she was better. Not only did Rosie learn how to dance, but she also learned to control her body and stay still when necessary. She concentrated better in class, did not distract others, and handled other tasks adequately.

THE END.

KIDS MUST NEVER MAKE MISTAKES!

Once upon a time, there lived a girl named Lottie. Lottie was smart and loved to have fun. She loved to draw and paint. One day, Lottie was drawing with a pencil in an arts class when she saw that she had not correctly drawn the butterfly's wings.

As she erased the wings so she could redraw them, Charlie, who was also drawing beside her, stopped her. 'You are not to erase anything,' he said. 'I have to; I made a mistake with the wings; I need to correct it,' she said. 'Don't let the arts teacher hear you; mistakes are not allowed. Don't you know that kids must never make mistakes?' he asked her.

'I don't think that is true. I made some mistakes; once I mistakenly dropped an egg, it broke; mom was not mad at me,' Lottie said.

'Kids are not allowed to make mistakes, and if you make more mistakes in arts, you will never be a good artist,' he told her. Lottie thought about what he had said.

She did not complete the drawing and stopped attending arts class. She kept making excuses when it was time for arts because she was scared of making mistakes.

Whenever she was home, she would keep to herself and be very careful whenever she was doing anything.

One day, the arts teacher called Lottie, 'why have you stopped coming to arts class?' he asked her. 'Nothing, I have been busy with basketball,' she said. 'Tell me the truth, Lottie. I know you don't play basketball,' he said. 'I am scared of making mistakes, and if I keep making mistakes, I will never be good enough,' she said.

'That is not true; mistakes do not define you. Instead, he told her that we are meant to learn from our mistakes to do better.' Lottie was happy she could draw again; she was no longer scared of making mistakes; whenever she made mistakes, she learned from them so she would not repeat the same error.

THE END.

If you found this storybook helpful or inspiring, please spare me two minutes of your valuable time to leave an honest review on my Amazon page on how your child found this book. Were they inspired? What thoughts were triggered as they went through the different stories?
I look forward to hearing your thoughts.
Many thanks

lease check out my other books for kids available on Amazon:

- Awesome Princesses, Mermaids & Unicorns Coloring Book For Kids
- Amazing Dinosaur Alphabet Coloring Book For Kids
- The Cutest Pet Animals Coloring Book For Kids
- Super Awesome Kids: 25 Inspiring Short Stories Of Awesome Boys and Girls About Kindness, Growth Mindset, Mindfulness, Confidence and Courage

THANK YOU :-)

Made in United States
Orlando, FL
02 December 2022

25421648R00041